WW84

WONDER WOMAN DC

TRUTH,
LOVE &
WONDER

INSPIRATIONAL QUOTES & STORIES FROM WONDER WOMAN

WRITTEN BY ALEXANDRA WEST

TRUTH, LOVE

STORY BY PATTY JENKINS AND GEOFF JOHNS

INSPIRATIONAL QUOTES & STORIES

20 21 22 23 24   PC/LSCC   10 9 8 7 6 5 4 3 2 1   FIRST EDITION

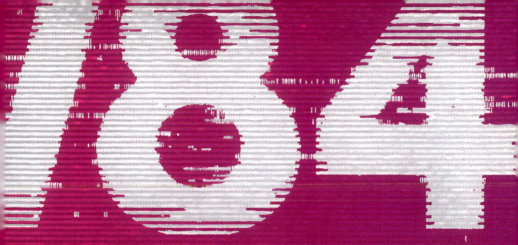

1984

WONDER WOMAN

WONDER WOMAN CREATED BY WILLIAM MOULTON MARSTON

& WONDER

FROM WONDER WOMAN

SCREENPLAY BY PATTY JENKINS, GEOFF JOHNS, AND DAVID CALLAHAM

HARPER

An Imprint of HarperCollinsPublishers

E N T S

184

WONDER WOMAN

.... Introduction ....

.... Truth ....

.... Love ....

.... Wonder ....

PLEASE JUST CALL ME DIANA.

AFTER ALL, IT LOOKS LIKE WE ARE GOING TO BE CLOSE FRIENDS ONCE YOU FINISH READING THROUGH MY JOURNAL. WE MIGHT AS WELL GET THE FANCY TITLES OUT OF THE WAY. DID YOU KNOW THAT THEY'VE TAKEN TO CALLING ME WONDER WOMAN IN THE NEWS? OF COURSE, I FIND THIS VERY FLATTERING BUT IT'S ALSO MADE ME THINK ABOUT THE WORD "WONDER." WHAT DOES IT ACTUALLY MEAN TO ME? WHAT DOES THIS SUPER HERO "WONDER WOMAN" STAND FOR?

UPON REFLECTION OF MY EXPERIENCES HERE IN MAN'S WORLD, I'VE REALIZED THAT I'VE LIVED MY LIFE BY SEEKING TRUTH, FINDING LOVE, AND NOW . . . APPRECIATING WONDER.

WHAT DOES THAT ALL MEAN EXACTLY? WELL . . .YOU'LL SEE.

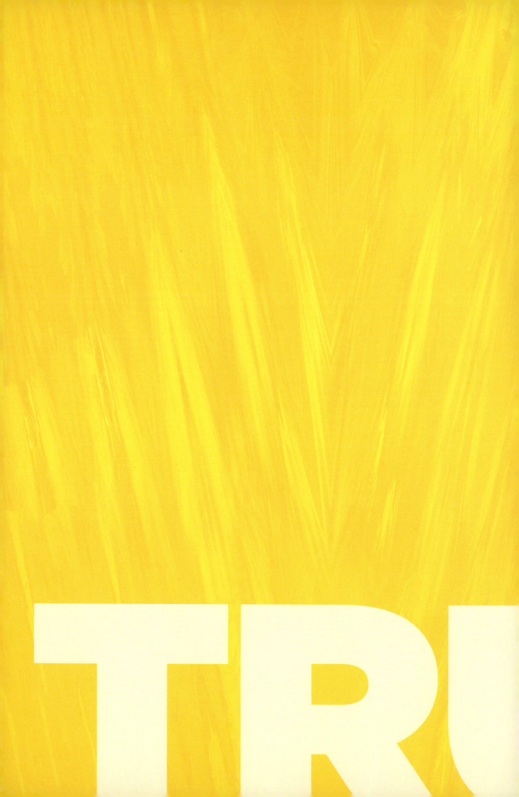

WONDER WOMAN

"THIS WORLD

WAS A BEAUTIFUL PLACE
AND YOU CANNOT
YOU CAN ONLY HAVE
AND THE TRUTH

THE

JUST AS IT WAS.
HAVE IT ALL.
THE TRUTH.
IS ENOUGH.
TRUTH IS
BEAUTIFUL."

YOUNG PRINCESS DIANA
Ready to compete in the
Amazon Games and accept the
truth when confronted with it.

I LEARNED MY LESSON
THE HARD WAY, A LONG, LONG
TIME AGO—AND NOW I WILL
NEVER BE THE SAME.

IT SHOULD BE SIMPLE—
JUST TELL THE TRUTH.
NEVER LIE. NEVER DECEIVE.
THIS IS A LESSON I LEARNED
AS A CHILD AND A CODE
I HAVE TRIED TO LIVE MY
LIFE BY EVERY DAY.

BUT . . . SOMETIMES
THE TRUTH IS COMPLICATED.
SOMETIMES THE TRUTH
IS DANGEROUS.

CAN YOU THINK
OF A TIME WHEN YOUR
TRUTH WAS A BIT
COMPLICATED?

"THE
TRUTH
BIGGER

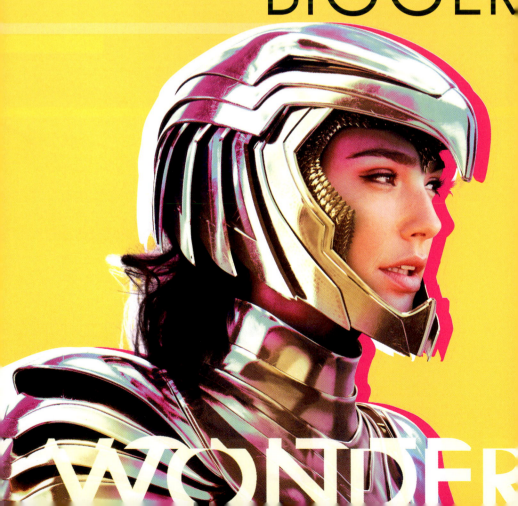

WONDER

IS
THAN ALL OF
US."

WOMAN

WHEN I WAS A SMALL CHILD LIVING ON THE HIDDEN ISLAND OF THEMYSCIRA WITH THE AMAZONS, THERE WAS A COMPETITION EVERY YEAR CALLED THE AMAZON GAMES. IT WAS DESIGNED TO DETERMINE THE MOST POWERFUL WARRIOR AMONG US. ONE YEAR, IT WAS FINALLY MY TURN TO COMPETE. ALTHOUGH I WAS YOUNG, THE YOUNGEST OF ALL THE COMPETITORS, I WAS DETERMINED TO PROVE MYSELF.

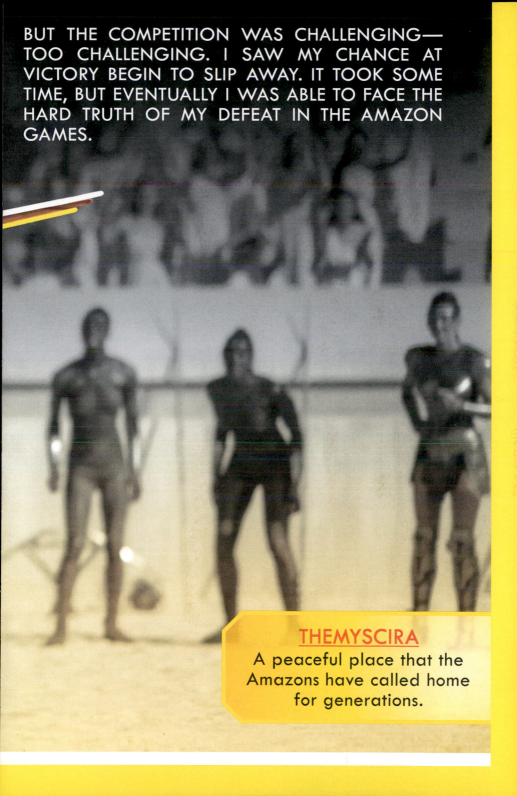

BUT THE COMPETITION WAS CHALLENGING—TOO CHALLENGING. I SAW MY CHANCE AT VICTORY BEGIN TO SLIP AWAY. IT TOOK SOME TIME, BUT EVENTUALLY I WAS ABLE TO FACE THE HARD TRUTH OF MY DEFEAT IN THE AMAZON GAMES.

THEMYSCIRA
A peaceful place that the Amazons have called home for generations.

"**WHAT** WHEN FACED **TRUTH** THAN YOU'D

WONDER

ONE DOES WITH THE IS MORE **DIFFICULT THINK."**

WOMAN

MY PEOPLE, THE AMAZONS,
ARE THE KEEPERS OF A TOOL CALLED
THE LASSO OF HESTIA.

THE LASSO OF HESTIA **COMPELS ONE TO TELL THE TRUTH**. MY PEOPLE HAVE MADE USE OF IT FOR CENTURIES. IT IS NOT TO BE USED LIGHTLY. TO FORCE SOMEONE TO SPEAK THE TRUTH, WITHOUT THEIR CONSENT, SHOULD NEVER BE PREFERRED TO THE TRUTH SPOKEN FREELY. UNFORTUNATELY, MY PEOPLE HAVE NEEDED TO USE THE LASSO OF HESTIA AT TIMES TO KEEP OURSELVES SAFE FROM HARM.

THINK OF WHAT DAMAGE COULD BE DONE IF THE LASSO OF HESTIA FELL INTO THE WRONG HANDS.

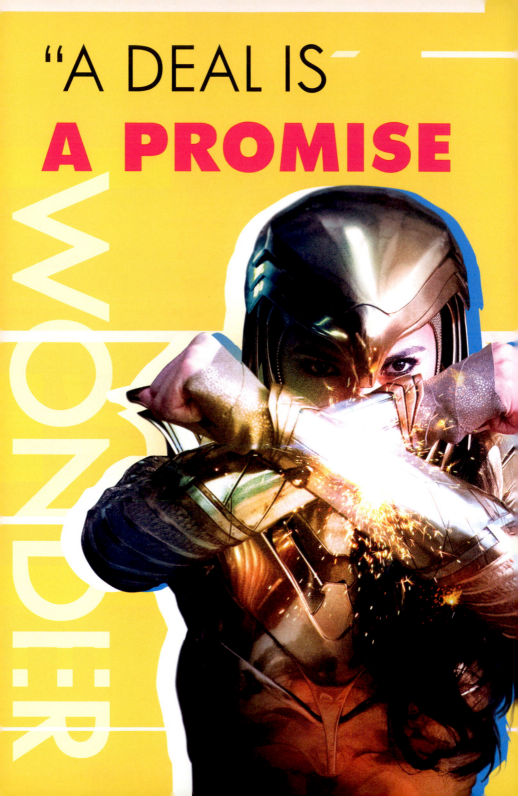

"A DEAL IS **A PROMISE**

WONDER

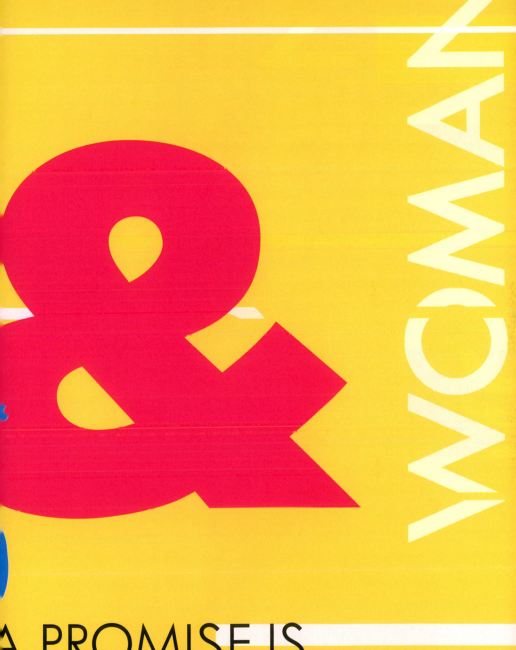

&

WOMAN

A PROMISE IS
UNBREAKABLE."

MANY PEOPLE HAVE NO IDEA WHAT **THE TRUE IDENTITY** IS OF THE PERSON THEY ONLY KNOW AS WONDER WOMAN. ALTHOUGH TRUTH IS FUNDAMENTALLY VALUABLE TO ME, STILL I AM COMPELLED TO KEEP THIS TRUTH HIDDEN FROM MOST. WHEN I DOUBT THIS DECISION I HAVE MADE, I REMIND MYSELF WHAT IS TRULY ON THE LINE.

WITHOUT MY IDENTITY HIDDEN, I WOULD BE UNABLE TO PROTECT PEOPLE THE WAY THAT I DO. IT IS ONLY TO KEEP OTHERS SAFE THAT I KEEP THIS SECRET. BUT I KNOW MYSELF, AND **I KNOW MY TRUTH**.

ARES, THE GOD OF WAR, ONCE TRIED TO CONVINCE ME TO REJECT THE THINGS I BELIEVED TO BE TRUE. HE TRIED TO CONVINCE ME THAT I WAS WRONG TO BELIEVE THAT HUMANKIND WAS WORTH SAVING, WORTH PROTECTING. ARES LIED TO ME.

CHOOSE... LOVE

HE SAID THAT HE WAS NOT THE GOD OF WAR,
BUT THE GOD OF TRUTH. HE ASKED ME TO JOIN
HIM IN THE DESTRUCTION. BUT THE TRUTH IS . . .
WHEN PEOPLE CHOOSE LOVE OVER HATE
AND CHAOS, THERE IS NOTHING MORE
POWERFUL ON THIS EARTH.

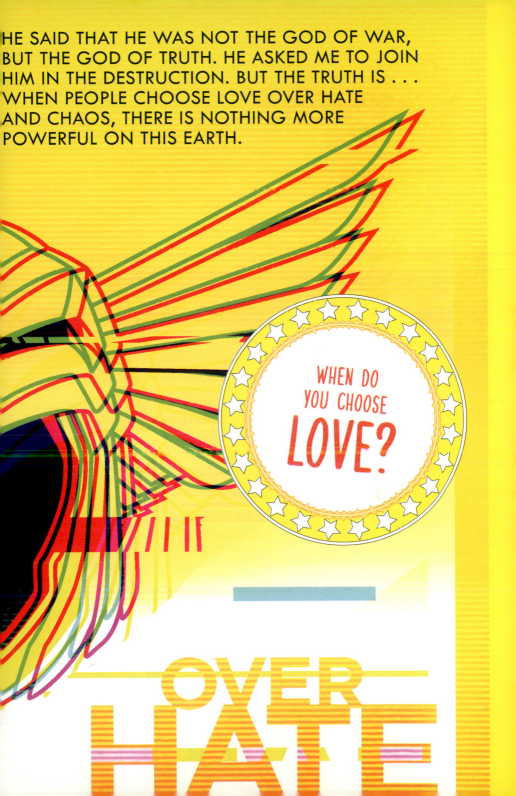

WHEN DO
YOU CHOOSE
LOVE?

OVER
HATE

"I USED TO WANT TO SAVE THE WORLD. TO END WAR AND BRING PEACE TO MANKIND; BUT THEN I GLIMPSED THE **DARKNESS** THAT LIVES WITHIN THEIR LIGHT.

I LEARNED THAT INSIDE EVERY ONE OF THEM THERE WILL ALWAYS BE BOTH. THE **CHOICE** EACH MUST MAKE FOR THEMSELVES—SOMETHING NO HERO WILL EVER **DEFEAT**."

CHOOSE TO FIGHT BACK
Wonder Woman heads to the mall
to confront the bad guys.

INSIDE EVERY PERSON, THERE IS THE POWER TO CHOOSE TO BE A HERO OR BE A VILLAIN. YOU NEED TO CHOOSE. NO ONE ELSE CAN MAKE THAT CHOICE FOR YOU.

AS FOR WHAT I CHOOSE . . . I CHOOSE TO STAY, I CHOOSE TO FIGHT, AND I CHOOSE TO GIVE, FOR THE WORLD I KNOW CAN BE. NOW, I CHOOSE TO HELP THE WORLD SAVE ITSELF. THAT'S THE TRUTH.

MOTHER'S COMFORT
Diana's mother comforts her
after the young girl's defeat
at the Amazon games.

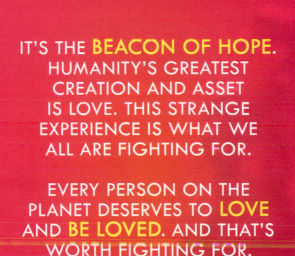

IT'S THE **BEACON OF HOPE.**
HUMANITY'S GREATEST
CREATION AND ASSET
IS LOVE. THIS STRANGE
EXPERIENCE IS WHAT WE
ALL ARE FIGHTING FOR.

EVERY PERSON ON THE
PLANET DESERVES TO **LOVE**
AND **BE LOVED.** AND THAT'S
WORTH FIGHTING FOR.

"ONE DAY YOU WILL ALL OF THE YOU DREAM **AND** HIPPO

BECOME
THINGS
OF AND MORE.
EVERYTHING
WILL BE DIFFERENT."

STRE

MY FIRST EXPERIENCE WITH LOVE WAS THE LOVE I HAD FROM MY **MOTHER**. LOVE TAKES MANY FORMS AND FOR MY MOTHER, WELL . . . SOME MIGHT CALL IT **TOUGH LOVE**. SHE GAVE ME IMPORTANT GUIDANCE AND HELPED ME THROUGH MY MOST DIFFICULT CHALLENGES. ALTHOUGH IT MAY HAVE SEEMED TOUGH ON THE OUTSIDE AND I MIGHT HAVE FELT FRUSTRATED AT SUCH A YOUNG AGE, I KNOW NOW THAT EVERYTHING SHE DID FOR ME SHE DID BECAUSE SHE LOVED ME.

SHE WAS AND STILL IS THE **STRONGEST** PERSON I KNOW. ALTHOUGH I KNOW THAT MY PLACE IS HERE AMONG HUMANS, I FIND MYSELF MISSING HER IN THE SMALL QUIET MOMENTS.

HIPPOLYTA

Queen of the Amazons
and ruler of Themyscira.

MY AUNT,

ANTIOPE

SPEAKING OF STRONG . . .

MY AUNT, ANTIOPE, WAS A MAJOR INFLUENCE ON MY LIFE. SHE WAS SORT OF LIKE A BIG SISTER. OK, MAYBE SOMETIMES SHE WAS LIKE A SECOND MOM. AFTER HER PASSING, I WAS LEFT WONDERING WHAT I WAS GOING TO DO WITHOUT HER GUIDANCE. WE LOVED EACH OTHER FIERCELY, AND THAT STRONG BOND WAS THE LEGACY SHE LEFT ME. TO SHARE YOUR HEART WITH SOMEONE SO BOUNDLESSLY IS SOMETHING THAT STAYS WITH YOU EVEN WHEN THAT PERSON IS GONE.

"NO
TRUE
IS BORN

ANT

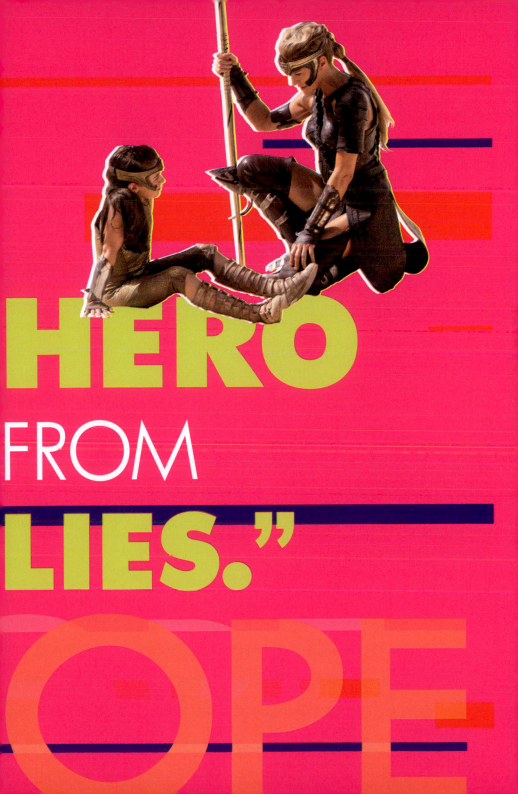

YOUNG
PRINCESS
DIANA

GROWING UP,

I LIVED IN AWE OF **THE AMAZING WOMEN** AROUND ME. MY MOTHER, QUEEN HIPPOLYTA. MY AUNT, HER GENERAL. I HAD THE GOOD FORTUNE OF GROWING UP SURROUNDED BY POWERFUL, BRILLIANT PEOPLE. IT WAS MY GREATEST **HONOR** TO LIVE AND WORK BY THEIR SIDE.

I TRAINED HARD TO PROVE **MY WORTH** AS AN AMAZON. FOR A TIME, I FELT I WOULD NEVER BE AS STRONG AS I NEEDED TO BE. IN FACT, I STILL FEEL THAT WAY . . .

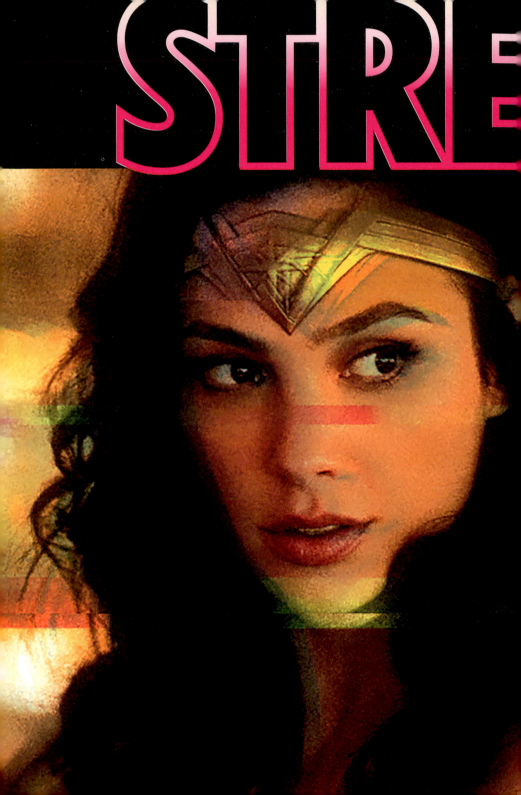

IN MY MOMENTS OF DOUBT,
I REMEMBER WHAT MY AUNT
ONCE SAID TO ME.

"YOU ARE
STRONGER
THAN YOU
BELIEVE.
YOU HAVE
GREATER
POWERS
THAN YOU
KNOW."

THE WORDS MY AUNT SPOKE THAT DAY WERE **TRUE** IN MORE WAYS THAN I COULD KNOW. LITTLE DID I KNOW THAT DAY THAT MY LIFE WOULD CHANGE. I WOULD **MEET** A STRANGE, WONDERFUL PERSON NAMED STEVE TREVOR. I WOULD LEAVE MY HOME AND EVERYTHING I KNEW TO SERVE AND **SAVE A WORLD** I DIDN'T YET KNOW EXISTED.

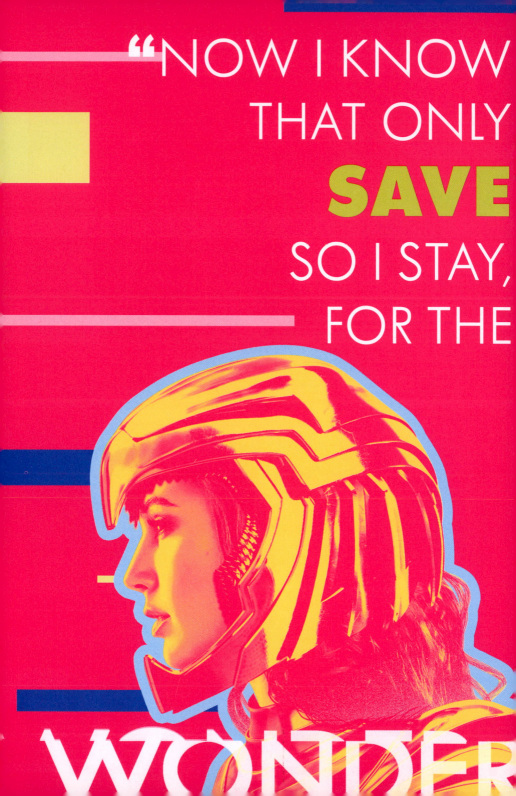

"NOW I KNOW THAT ONLY **SAVE** SO I STAY, FOR THE

WONDER

LOVE CAN TRULY

THE WORLD.

I FIGHT, AND I GIVE,
WORLD I KNOW

CAN BE."

IN A STRANGE TIME IN MY LIFE, I FELL **MADLY IN LOVE** WITH SOMEONE. ISN'T FALLING IN LOVE STRANGE IN AND OF ITSELF? MY LOVE FOR **STEVE TREVOR** CREPT INTO MY HEART LIKE A FOG ROLLING IN OVER THE MOUNTAINS OF THEMYSCIRA. OUR TIME SPENT **TOGETHER** IN THE WAR BONDED US FOR LIFE. THERE'S NO QUESTION ABOUT THAT. SINCE I LOST HIM, I FOUND MY **HEART** ACHING. LIKE SOMETHING WAS MISSING. NOW HE IS BACK. NOW WE ARE TOGETHER AGAIN. NOW SOMETHING THAT WAS MISSING HAS BEEN **FOUND**.

STEVE TREVOR

Out of space and time, Steve tries to make sense of his new world.

"I WISH WE HAD MORE TIME. I LOVE YOU."

I THOUGHT THAT THOSE WERE THE LAST WORDS I WAS EVER GOING TO HEAR FROM STEVE. I KEPT THE WATCH HE GAVE ME. I CARRIED IT CLOSE TO MY HEART FOR MANY YEARS. I STILL PINCH MYSELF WHEN I SEE HIM THESE DAYS. WE FINALLY GOT THE TIME HE WISHED FOR . . . WE WISHED FOR.

"THE WORLD

STEVE

"NEEDS YOU."

TREVOR

I APPRECIATE EVERY MOMENT.

BEING THAT I DON'T AGE, MY LIFE TENDS TO BE MARKED WITH LOSS. I STILL FONDLY REMEMBER THE FRIENDS I'VE LOST OVER THE YEARS. NOT ALL OF THE FRIENDS WERE LOST DUE TO TRAGEDY, BUT AS TIME WENT ON THEY GREW OLDER AND I STAYED THE SAME AGE. ONE FRIEND IN PARTICULAR, STEVE'S SECRETARY, ETTA CANDY, COMES TO MIND.

THOUGH KIND-NATURED, SHE—AND I QUOTE— WOULD "NEVER BE OPPOSED TO ENGAGING IN A BIT OF FISTICUFFS." MEMORIES OF ETTA POP INTO MY HEAD EVERY NOW AND THEN. AND I SMILE BECAUSE I'M GRATEFUL FOR THE TIME WE HAD.

WHO ARE YOU GRATEFUL FOR?

I HAVE A FRIEND AT WORK. SHE STRUGGLED A LOT
WITH HER CONFIDENCE. IT WAS ALMOST AS IF SHE
WAS AFRAID TO BE HERSELF. WHEN YOU FEEL
CONFIDENT IN YOURSELF, THE WORLD STARTS
TO LOOK LESS INTIMIDATING. WE EACH
HAVE OUR OWN UNIQUE STRENGTHS, AND
WHEN WE IDENTIFY THOSE STRENGTHS AND
BEGIN TO DEVELOP THEM, WE CAN SET
OURSELVES UP FOR A STRONGER
SENSE OF SELF.

A NEW FRIENDSHIP

Diana and Dr. Barbara Minerva run
into each other at work. Literally.

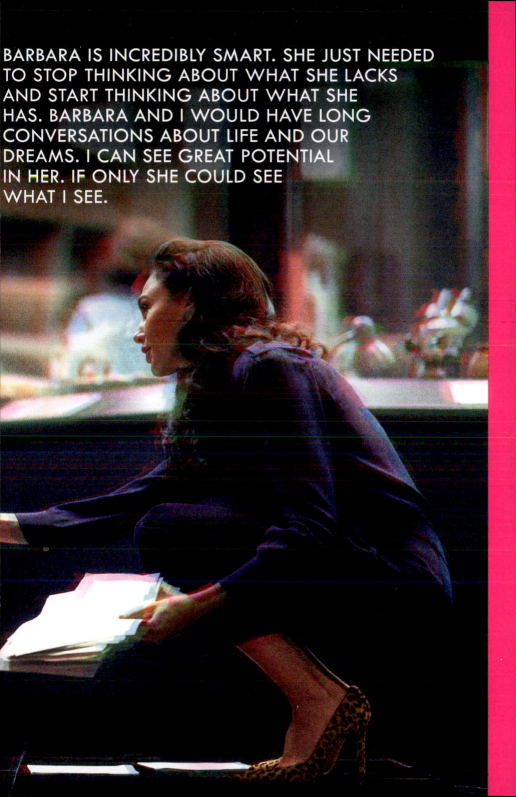

BARBARA IS INCREDIBLY SMART. SHE JUST NEEDED TO STOP THINKING ABOUT WHAT SHE LACKS AND START THINKING ABOUT WHAT SHE HAS. BARBARA AND I WOULD HAVE LONG CONVERSATIONS ABOUT LIFE AND OUR DREAMS. I CAN SEE GREAT POTENTIAL IN HER. IF ONLY SHE COULD SEE WHAT I SEE.

"YOU ARE STRONGER

YOU HAVE

ANT

THAN YOU BELIEVE. GREATER POWERS

THAN YOU

KNOW."

FEAR CAN BE JUST AS **POWERFUL** AS LOVE. INSTEAD OF TURNING TO LOVE, BARBARA TURNED TO FEAR. SHE FOUND ANOTHER WAY TO MAKE THE WORLD LESS INTIMIDATING. SHE BECAME A COMPLETELY DIFFERENT PERSON.

THERE IS ONLY ONE PERSON IN THE WORLD THAT CAN BE YOU. WHY WASTE YOUR TIME BEING SOMEONE ELSE? BE KIND TO YOURSELF. IN TIMES OF SELF-DOUBT, REMIND YOURSELF OF YOUR **SUCCESSES** RATHER THAN YOUR LOSSES. INSTEAD OF DECIDING THAT SHE WASN'T GOOD ENOUGH, BARBARA COULD'VE BEEN STRONG ENOUGH TO FIND THE GOOD IN HERSELF. THAT'S **TRUE POWER**.

THE COMFORT OF LOVE
Diana feels the most like herself when she's surrounded by the ones she loves, like Steve.

LOVE

WE HAVE **THE POWER TO EXPRESS** LOVE FOR OTHERS. THEY COULD BE FRIENDS, FAMILY, OR EVEN STRANGERS. BUT THE ONE MOST PEOPLE TEND TO FORGET ABOUT IS **LOVE FOR YOURSELF.** IF YOU CAN'T SPEAK KINDLY TO YOURSELF, IF YOU CAN'T CONNECT WITH THE PERSON YOU SEE IN THE MIRROR, THEN IT INHIBITS YOUR ABILITY TO LOVE OTHERS.

LOVING YOURSELF IS THE MOST **COURAGEOUS** THING ANYBODY CAN DO. ONCE YOU DO THAT, IT OPENS THE DOOR TO LOVE OTHERS.

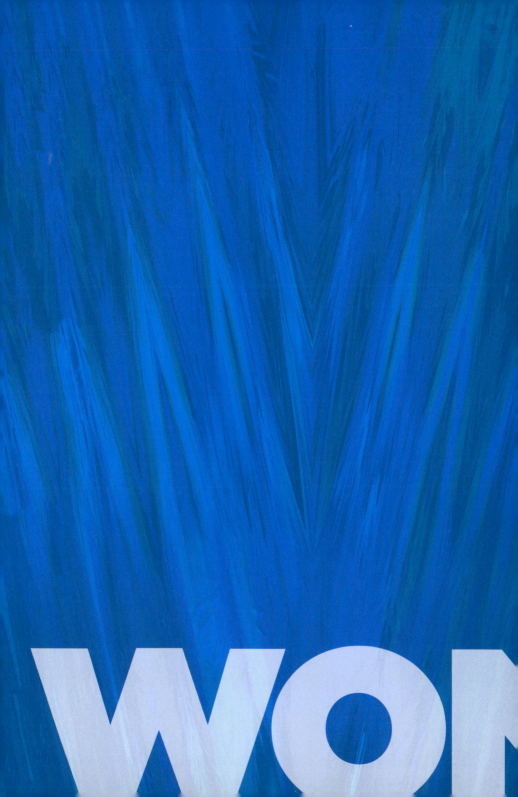

REMEMBER MY NAME
Diana works hard to uphold
her title as Wonder Woman.

I AM KNOWN TO MANY
AS WONDER WOMAN.
OR THE WOMAN OF WONDER.
THIS MONIKER WAS GIVEN TO
ME WHEN MY WORK BEGAN TO
GAIN MORE RECOGNITION IN THE
WORLD. PERHAPS SOME PEOPLE
SAW A WOMAN WHO HAD THE
POWERS TO DEFEND THE WEAK
FROM PAIN AND INJUSTICE,
AND THOUGHT THAT WAS
A THING OF WONDER.

FOR MY PART, THE NAME
WILL FOREVER REMIND ME
OF THE WONDER I TAKE IN
THE WORLD AROUND ME.

WHAT DO YOU
SEE IN THE WORLD
THAT YOU THINK IS
WONDERFUL?

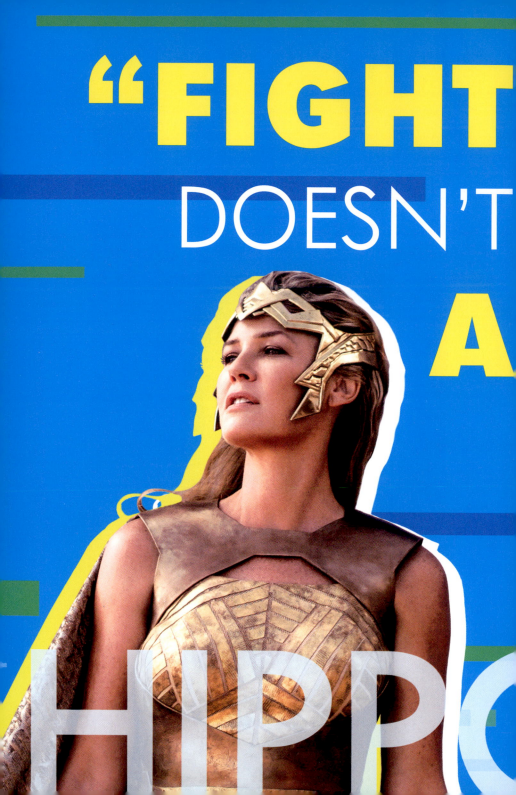

THERE ARE BAD PEOPLE IN THIS WORLD. AND THERE ALWAYS WILL BE. I UNDERSTAND THAT NOW. WHEN I SEE EVIL IN THE WORLD, I TRY TO NOT LET ANGER CONTROL ME. INSTEAD I FOCUS ON A MORE POSITIVE MOTIVATION TO PROJECT ME FORWARD. **DEFIANCE.**

MAXWELL LORD

This con man's greatest desire is money, but that will be his downfall too.

ONCE I SAW THE WORLD,

FILLED WITH SO MANY DIFFERENT PEOPLE AND WAYS OF LIFE, I KNEW MY PURPOSE.

I KNEW IF NO ONE ELSE WOULD DEFEND THE WORLD AGAINST EVIL, THEN I MUST.

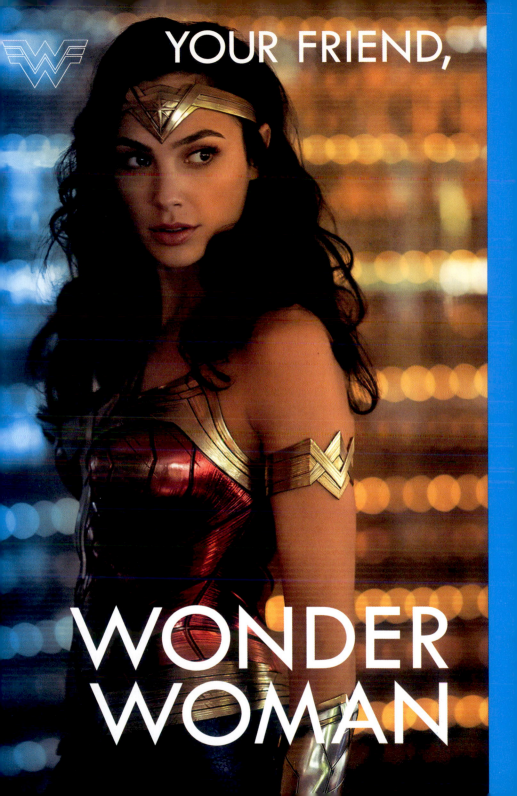

POWER

WITH THE **STRENGTH** AND **POWER**
OF A GODDESS . . .

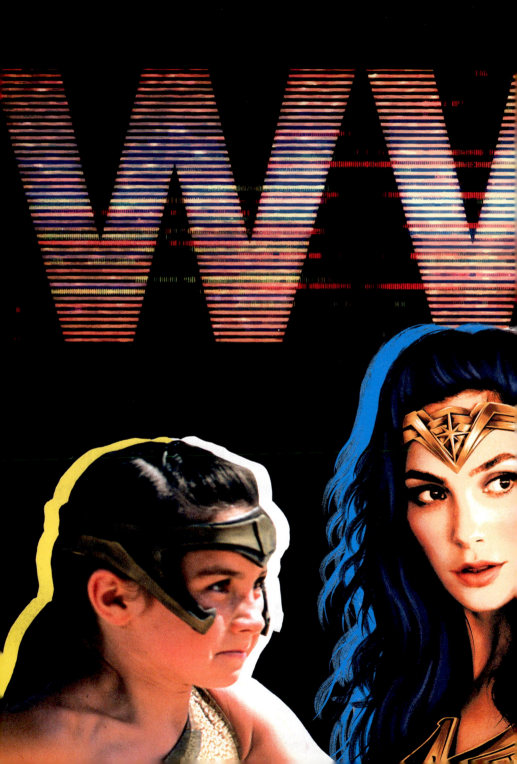

. . . AND THE HEART AND MIND OF A HUMAN, I BECAME WONDER WOMAN TO THIS WORLD.

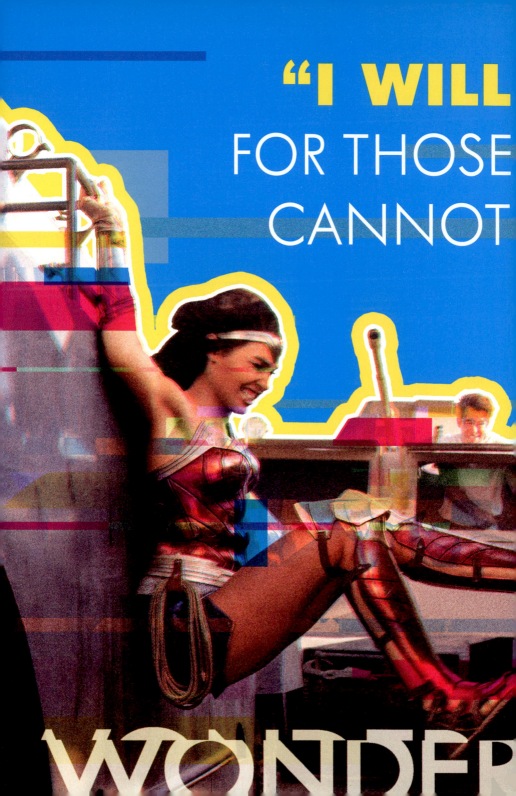

FIGHT
WHO
FIGHT FOR
THEMSELVES."

WOMAN

MY
EXPERIENCES

HERE AWAY FROM THEMYSCIRA HAVE CHANGED ME INSIDE AND OUT. THE PURE HEARTS I'VE FOUND, THE INNOCENCE I'VE SEEN, THE LOVE I'VE FELT . . . THESE MOMENTS HAVE ALL CONTRIBUTED TO THIS LARGER EXPERIENCE. A *HUMAN* EXPERIENCE.

BECAUSE NONE OF THESE THINGS CAN HAPPEN WITHOUT ALSO EXPERIENCING **THE DARKNESS**. BUT THAT MAKES SEEING SOMEONE FIND THE PATH OF TRUTH, LOVE, AND **WONDER** THAT MUCH SWEETER.

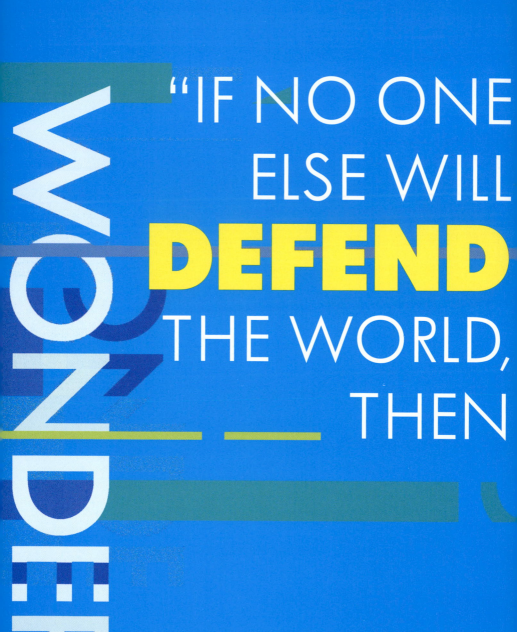

WONDER

"IF NO ONE ELSE WILL **DEFEND** THE WORLD, THEN

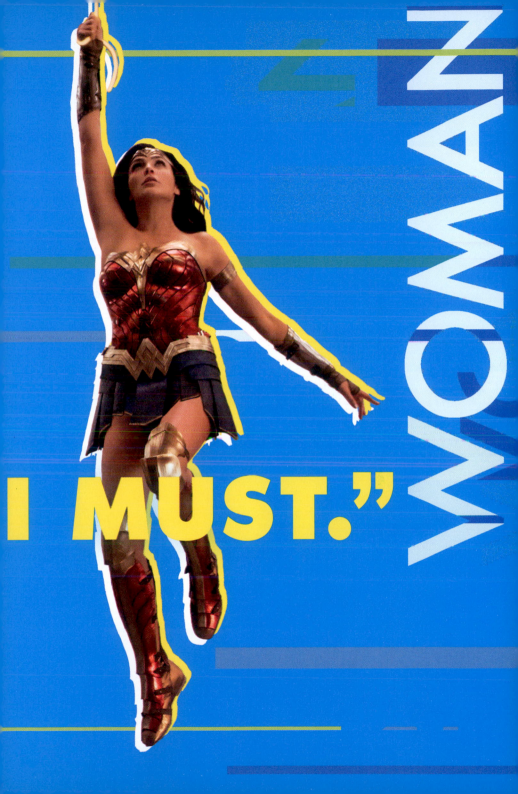

I SEEK PEACE. BUT WHEN A FIGHT ARRIVES, I CAN FIGHT.

I AM AND ALWAYS WILL BE A WARRIOR. MY MOTHER'S DAUGHTER.

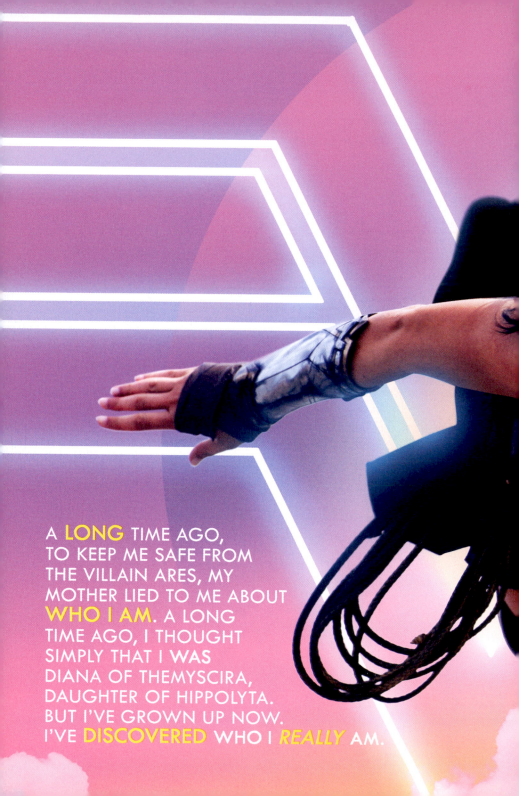

A **LONG** TIME AGO, TO KEEP ME SAFE FROM THE VILLAIN ARES, MY MOTHER LIED TO ME ABOUT **WHO I AM**. A LONG TIME AGO, I THOUGHT SIMPLY THAT I WAS DIANA OF THEMYSCIRA, DAUGHTER OF HIPPOLYTA. BUT I'VE GROWN UP NOW. I'VE **DISCOVERED** WHO I *REALLY* AM.

I AM
TRUTH.

I AM
LOVE.

I AM
WONDER.

WHAT ARE
YOU?

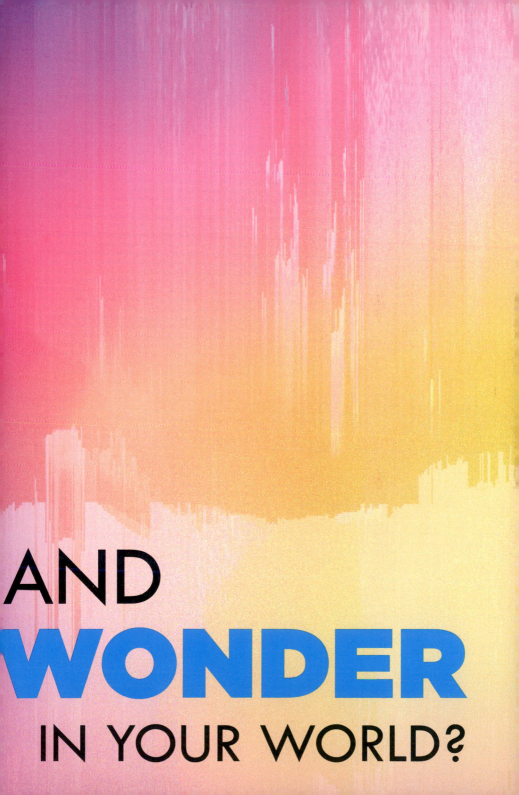

AND WONDER
IN YOUR WORLD?